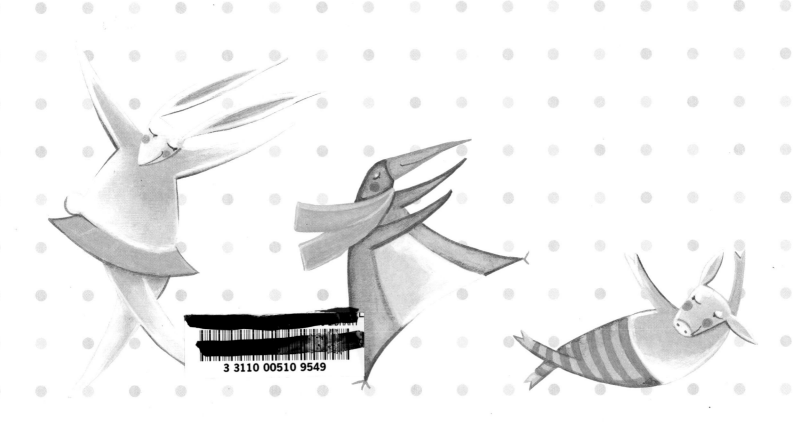

The Three Funny Friends

● ● ●

The Three Funny Friends

by Charlotte Zolotow
Illustrated by Linda Bronson

• • •

Running Press
KIDS
PHILADELPHIA · LONDON

Text © 2003, 1961 by Charlotte Zolotow
Illustrations © 2003 by Linda Bronson

Printed in China

9   8   7   6   5   4   3   2   1
Digit on the right indicates the number of this printing

Library of Congress Control Number: 2002095671

ISBN 0-7624-1553-3

Designed by Frances J. Soo Ping Chow
Acquired by Patty Aitken Smith
Edited by Patty Aitken Smith and Susan K. Hom
Typography: Sassoon Infant and Sassoon Sans

This book may be ordered by mail from the publisher.
Please include $2.50 for postage and handling.
But try your bookstore first!

Published by Running Press Kids, an imprint of
Running Press Book Publishers
125 South Twenty-second Street
Philadelphia, Pennsylvania 19103-4399

Visit us on the web!
www.runningpress.com

For Rick and Susan Whelan, two good friends next door,
who are sometimes funny, but always really there

—C.Z.

To my father, with love

—L.B.

A little girl moved to a new town.

She didn't know any children there, but she wasn't lonely because she had three funny friends. Guy-guy, Bickerina, and Mr. Dobie. They were the three friends of the little girl in her new house.

But her mother never saw them. Her father never saw them.
Her brother never saw them.
It was funny.

Guy-guy did all sorts of things the little girl would **never** do.

He took the books out of the bookcase and scattered them all over the floor.

"Who did that?" the little girl's mother said. "Guy-guy," said the little girl.

But her mother couldn't see Guy-guy anywhere.

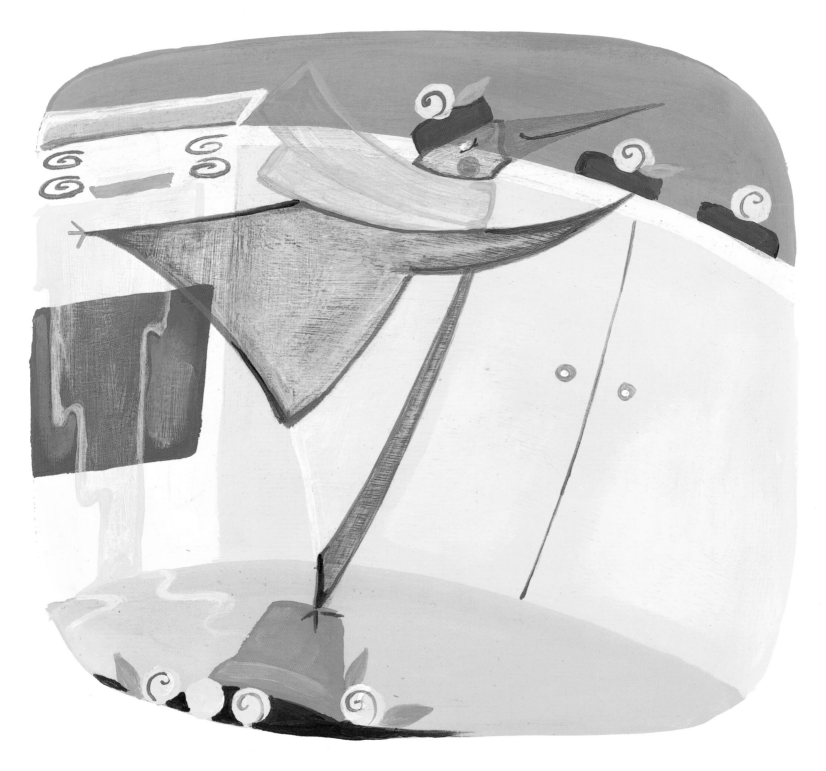

Guy-guy turned her mother's plant upside down to make pies.
He put the butter on top of the stove and the butter melted.

He tore the fringe off the mother's new curtains.

But when the little girl's mother said, "Who did this!" and the little girl said,

"Guy-guy," her mother could never see him anywhere.

Bickerina was different.

Bickerina did all sorts of things the little girl **wanted** to do:

"Bickerina bought you a castle, instead of this house,"

the little girl told her mother.

"Bickerina brought you a wild white horse," she said.

"Bickerina brought you a box full of beads," she said.

And when the little girl's mother was very tired, the little girl said,

"Never mind, Bickerina will help you. She will finish everything you have to do."

But the mother could never see Bickerina or the things that Bickerina did.

Mr. Dobie was special.

Mr. Dobie did things **instead** of the little girl.

When the little girl's mother said, "It's time for your bath,"

the little girl said, "Mr. Dobie took it for me."

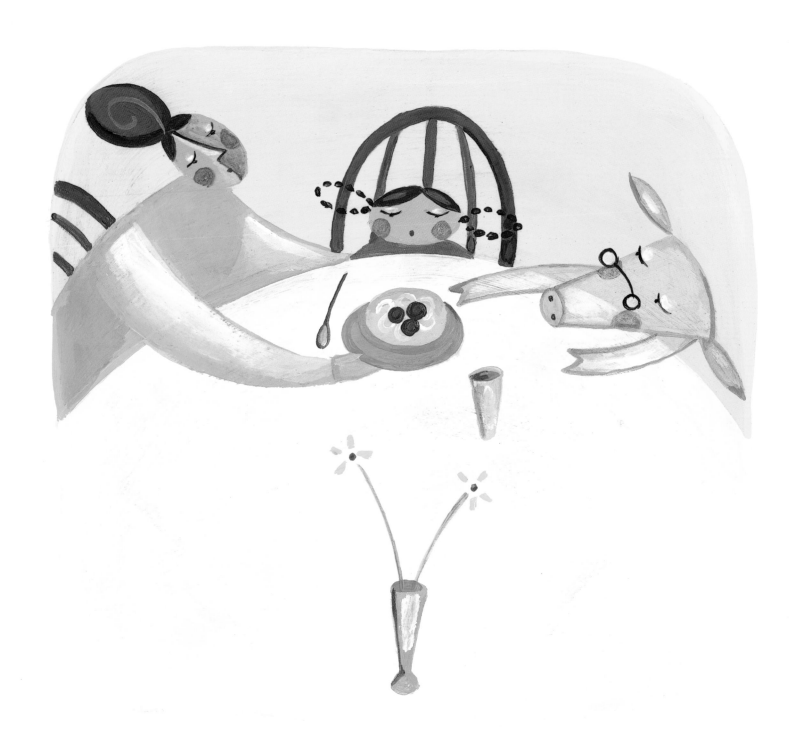

When the mother said, "Eat your supper," the little girl said,
"Mr. Dobie is eating it."

When the mother said, "It's time to go to bed," the little girl said,
"Mr. Dobie is sleeping for me." But the mother never saw Mr. Dobie.

Guy-guy, Bickerina, and Mr. Dobie.

They were the three friends of the little girl in her new house.

But her mother never saw them. Her father never saw them.

Her brother never saw them. It was funny.

Then one day the little girl met the little boy who lived next door.

His name was Tony.

She brought him in to meet her family. "This is my mother," she said.
And her mother saw Tony. "Hello," her mother said.
"This is my father," she said. And her father saw Tony. "Hello, Tony," he said.
"This is my brother," she said. "Hello," said her brother.
For they could really see that Tony was there.

And then the little girl began to play with Tony every day.

Sometimes the little girl and Tony broke things. Sometimes they messed things up.

And sometimes they brought real presents for the mother.

But what they broke they tried to fix. What they messed up they tried to clean up.

And what they brought the little girl's mother she could really see.

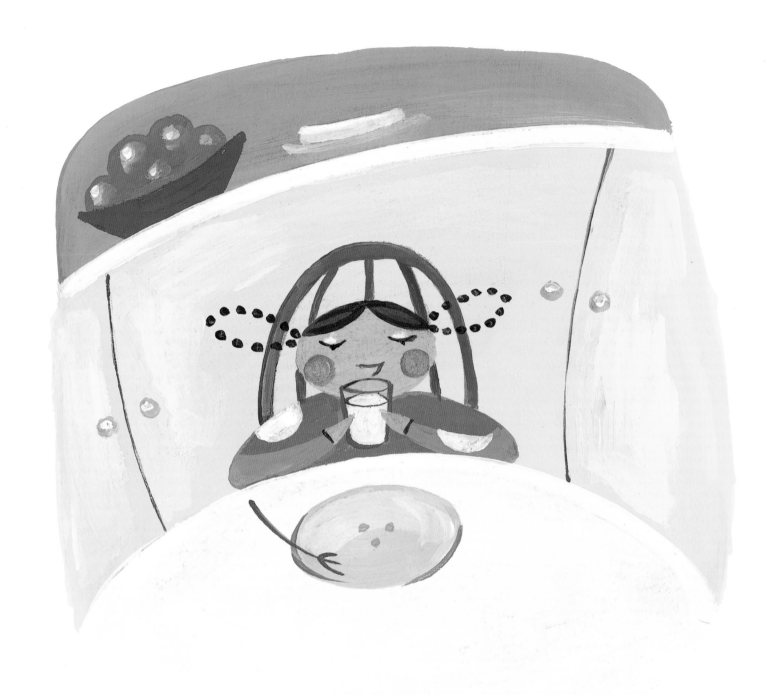

And the little girl was so happy she ate her own supper and drank her own milk

and took her own bath

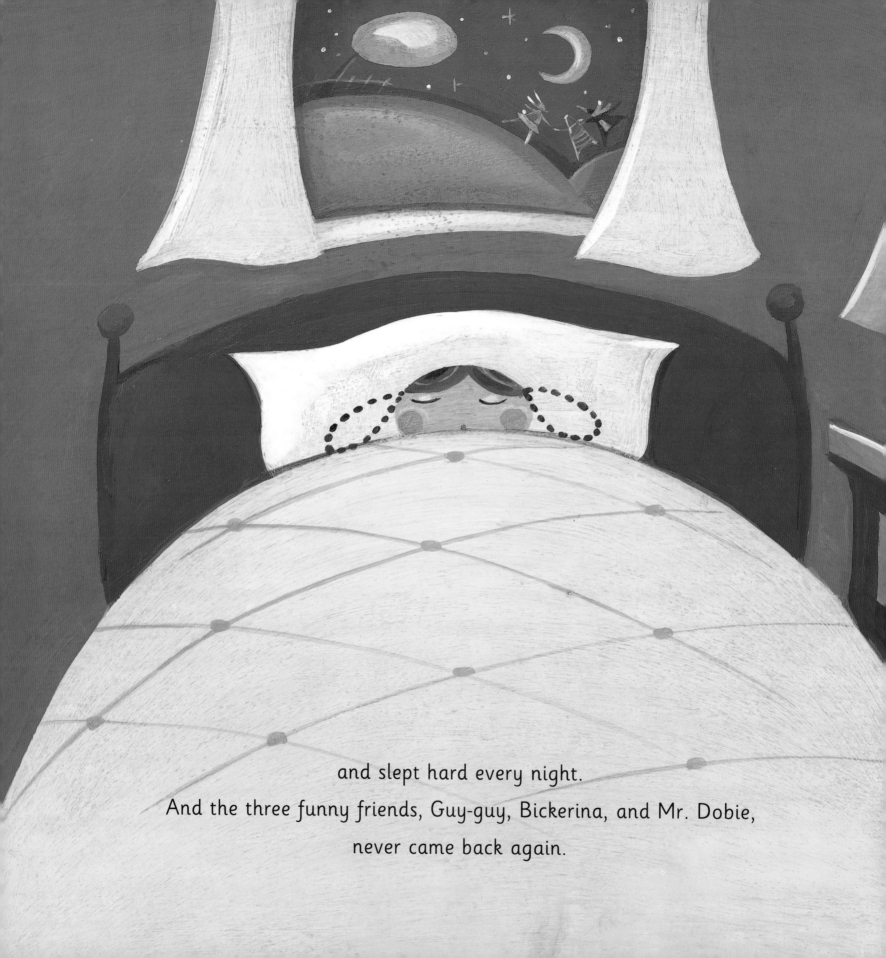

and slept hard every night.
And the three funny friends, Guy-guy, Bickerina, and Mr. Dobie,
never came back again.